The Pied Piper

My 1st Classic Story

a retelling by Eric Blair

illustrated by Ben Peterson

PICTURE WINDOW BOOKS
a capstone imprint

∽᳁

My First Classic Story is published by Picture Window Books
A Capstone Imprint
151 Good Counsel Drive, P.O. Box 669
Mankato, Minnesota 56002
www.capstonepub.com

Library of Congress Cataloging-in-Publication Data
Blair, Eric.
The Pied Piper / retold by Eric Blair ; illustrated by Ben Peterson.
p. cm. — (My first classic story)
Summary: The Pied Piper pipes a village free of rats,
and when the villagers refuse to pay him for the service
he pipes away their children as well.
ISBN 978-1-4048-6084-1 (library binding)
1. Pied Piper of Hamelin (Legendary character)—Legends.
[1. Pied Piper of Hamelin (Legendary character)—Legends.
2. Folklore—Germany.] I. Peterson, Ben, ill. II. Pied Piper of
Hamelin. English. III. Title.
PZ8.1.B5824Pi 2011
398.2—dc22
[E]   2010003626

Art Director: Kay Fraser
Graphic Designer: Emily Harris

∽᳁

The story of *The Pied Piper* has
been passed down for generations.
There are many versions of the story.
The following tale is a retelling of the
original version. While the story has
been cut for length and level, the basic
elements of the classic tale remain.

Long ago, millions of rats took over the town of Hamelin, Germany.

At first, the rats stayed under the streets.
But soon they became bolder.

The rats began to go into people's home.

The people were afraid.

Before long, rats were everywhere.
At night, they made so much noise
that no one could sleep.

The mayor called a meeting.

Suddenly, there was a knock at the door.
A stranger walked in.

The stranger was dressed in a funny coat.
He had a silver pipe around his neck.

"I understand that your town has a rat problem," said the stranger.

"It does," said the mayor.

"For a fee, I will get rid of the rats," said the stranger.

"If you can get rid of the rats, one thousand gold coins will be yours," the mayor said.

"Deal," said the stranger.

That night, the stranger stepped into the street. He began to play his pipe.

The rats came running.

They poured into the streets.

The stranger kept playing his silver pipe.

Then he marched toward the bridge.
When the stranger reached the middle
of the bridge, he raised his arm.

"Hippity-hop!" he cried.

All of the rats jumped into the river. At last, the king of the rats showed up.

The stranger asked, "Is that all of you?"

"Yes," the king rat said.

With that, the king threw himself from the bridge.

The next morning, the stranger found the mayor. "All of the rats are gone," he said. "It's time for you to pay me."

The mayor said, "We cannot pay you. We have no gold coins. The rats have destroyed our town."

The stranger became angry. Without a word, he stepped into the street. He began to play his pipe.

Children poured into the street.

The stranger marched out of town, playing his silver pipe as he went.

All of the children danced after him. When the stranger reached the mountain, it opened up.

The stranger and the children went inside. They were never seen again.